MW01248181

MANIFEST

BAVONNE

MANIFEST
come. sit down. let's talk...

Charleston, SC
www.PalmettoPublishing.com

MANIFEST

Come. Sit Down. Let's Talk...

First Edition

Paperback ISBN: 979-8-8229-0517-7

In memory of
Great-Great-Grandma Pine,
Great-Grandma Whitewater,
Grandpa Montiphus,
Great-Grandfather Bartholomew,
Great-Grandma Eretha,
Grandma Burnadine,
and
Grandma Stella

Dedicated to Father, who continuously protects my life and spiritual children unconventionally seeking God.

introduction

L adies and gentlemen, if you are lucky enough to love a man with your mind, certainly that is what you should do.

Come. Sit down. Let's talk.

Citta loved her man and the whole idea of intimacy. Citta loved that she had access to him but hated that he decided not to visit her every day. Or more than once a day, including overnight, for that matter. Knowing Citta would never be at the top of her game with the greatest mystery love of her life (by his choice, of course), something or someone had him locked into routine. It was obviously more important for him to be absent to her, but respectfully.

If he were a gangster with a camera on his house and loyalists who had taken an oath threatened his life, or he failed to come home on any night, the river might fill with cement shoes simply from smudged newspapers…

If he were the guardian of a young person who had to see him every night to understand his word, how his commitment is his bond, or how real love never fades…

Even if he had a woman at home as the meal and women on the side as snacks and he needed to be available to all because he stays hungry for hot toothpick samples to protect the family…

Citta understood. She was a good woman that way.

Her man played his cards close to his chest with a front-row seat to many in the struggle. If the palm reader/tarot psychic advised, "Vulnerability of business or lifestyle endangers loved ones. You can't elevate in wealth without experiencing the loss of a soul tie, nor can you rise to fame without personal sacrifice, including poverty," unquestionably Citta would reply, "Keep your distance. We cannot fall in love." It would make sense not to drop anchor in that sea of hearts.

If you, she, or any of us, for that matter, woke up every morning thinking about a good partner who believes you are the most deserving person playing your heart cheap to the highest bidder, you would want someone to step in. Walk you through the experience of better. Where to find it. How to obtain it or certainly apply it for clarity and confirmation for a peaceful day at work. It must be hard to honor the vow and do what must be done for the sake of having a successful family life or business.

Strangely enough, the man did not want to answer any questions or be any day in her romantic calendar. Thinking long and hard, the question arose, "Was he a guardian angel or simply indescribable?" Citta's personality went from a superficial fracture to full-blown split. She worried and, without wig or role play, Citta expressed, "We are not lovers, tangled in regrets, supportive in tone and word, respectful in deed. You, whom I invested my talents in, you made me who I am. You not trying to be seen with me, dream with me, manifest off paper. You not trying to string me out to an octave or chords of praise where I call on Jesus for a deeper experience of us. To know I am exclusively yours when men push up *is not* what you want. What I offered you was not good enough. You either don't want the title or don't care to wear the crown."

But clearly, this tantrum, like any other when your tongue is a sword, was never a good one to throw to argue with a man about your relationship with God.

3

He ignored her on purpose, knowing more about her than she ever revealed.

They say when Jesus returns, transformed by marriage, He will use *the woman*. Mary at the beginning, Mary at the end, and…

"…for God and the family, as the Master's wife and mistress, may you be blessed with authority, generations of respect, and manifest soul-saving power." — Citta

CHAPTER 1

be no longer still

You ever watch someone of the opposite sex and daydream? Not so much marriage but lust in mind, standing at a distance. They smell good. They look good, have perfect manners, own a pair of shoes, and can use a fork and knife at the fanciest place, which was probably a local steak-and-seafood diner.

How are you looking at a fine person when you are living an alternative lifestyle? You are attractive enough to tie cherry stems with your tongue, but you think about what you can get away with. Which friend can you trust long enough to have a romantic breakfast with for more than a month?

It was not easy being a family host. Don't ask me how; it wasn't exactly a college experiment.

But this man, OMG! Physically fit, he could run for miles. He was awesome in his awesomeness. His complexion was as flawless as chocolate coffee with milk. He could make you stand still and silently think things that would make you sin while licking your lips. I didn't know him, but the window-shop of him, the free glance, was all in the timing.

It had to be early. Around the time Mom needed to go on her to-do list of errands.

Citta took Mom on errands as a means to perfect driving. Buy some plants, a nonrusty nail from hardware. Groceries from a variety of stores. Every weekend was the same routine. In other words, there was no reason to sleep late. Stores opened near 7:00 a.m.

Driving and smiling with an alternative agenda, Citta searched. He was usually out at this time. "Come on; where are you?" And on some occasions, as her eyes saw him, she would twist her neck into what was short of an exorcism. No one knew his name or anything. His face was hidden by a hoodie most of the time, but he was everything perfect.

They say pastors' kids are the worst, but to be honest, 'tis true! We jump into stupid stuff, unable to swim with water up to our necks. We know God is real but wake day after day, fighting the call on our lives. You name it; we try it again and again. Again and again.

In Citta's case, thick church dirt and teary-eyed trial by the elders, or behaving like Mary before the rock toss, seemed to be excessive enough for life as a hermit. Lusting for a man she never met was nothing. The lessons in life teach us this: "Don't soul tie to folk to prove how sexy sexy is." There is always a possessive mind believing "If they can't have a perfect relationship or friendship, no one else should." It is almost as bad as doing business with a bad partner, but sometimes there is no one else to blame when you introduce yourself and sign up.

We all have these secrets that make us walking miracles. Now don't get me wrong. Young Citta's dark side was a horror. She got what she deserved, eventually. I mean, nobody wants to be at the table eating a snitch meal, and nobody wants a premature toe tag. We insure ourselves for over-the-shoulder glances just in case death comes knocking. Perhaps we escape soap-operatic illusions to get caught by accountability for character because when you come out the mud, ain't no pretend.

The brilliance in authenticity is the treasure of self-worth.

Love, no matter what day you look for it, is extremely hard to find, but we chase it. The high school sweetheart fairy tale that builds years, called anniversaries, is not in the skip-class or hooky playbook. The drug- or smoke-free spouse we encourage our innocent, test-stressed children to have is not exactly who or what we were.

The people we admired had their names stitched in the linings of fur coats. It is only after you mature beyond being called out by your name that you realize you are either wealthy with an umbilical cord wrapped around your neck or you are safely trapped and stuck in a magnetic nightmare where every day is groundhog familiar.

The world's frequency advanced, but the destination is up to us.

Society—pick any modern time—has weakened men who are not associated with the umbrella strength of unity. We've watered down wisdom. We've made women so strong they are brash, no longer emotional or believing in their natural beauty. In every other culture though, you open car doors, pull out chairs, don't raise your voice, and never cuss.

Young couples have not really seen *love* like our grandparents. You know, the man who wore a suit and hat on holidays. Covered his mouth, walking so you could not read his lips, or camouflaged his speech with a toothpick. The older empowered the younger, walking beside him or nodding the head, to signal approval or acknowledge presence. It was a tradition to be raised into manhood doing boy-to-man things. That concept left daughters with the impression that any boy becoming a man would protect her and cherish her as a gem, not a notch in his belt.

We think we know what men are made of. We expect them to roll out of bed superheroes, able to accomplish much with little help and no words of encouragement. We put upon them more than we care to admit, including belittling them for surviving day to day. We provide no role-model protection and no cause for unique participation. As women, we teach boys what we've seen men do, but we cannot teach them how to be men. DIY fishing and hunting skills only happen via private or lucky clusters. We know lack of communication decreases inspiration, but without leadership we become vulnerable to the cookie-cutter environment's structure.

Rephrased, we have wounded minds that habitually patch memory because there is no money in cures. If you control your mind, what goes in it or comes out your mouth, no door will consistently remain closed to you. You can jump up and down, preaching this in your home, but the deepest voice has the power, and for whatever reason, that is just how it is.

We have a generation of men missing from the lives of biological children. Men who are dads often date women and accept their child (or children). And in contrast, we have gentlemen who never fathered children giving their last names as fathers-in-love.

Daughters of absent fathers rarely seek affirmation. What they want is security from a tribal fortress with a mighty last name. Protection is often found in gangs, but even that family is not worry-free freedom. The branches of such trees are long, but the roots are not deep enough to provide water. Not even a tsunami can destroy a loving last name.

CHAPTER 2

won more day

Near the bus depot was a woman you only saw from the cashier counter up. She sold Dots, gumballs, Boston Baked Beans, Now and Later, Fire Stix, Red Hots, Orbits, and peppermints that melted on your tongue. Her candy was sweeter than Grandma's church-nurse candy. You know, the women who wear white on the front row and speak life? They distributed mints that put the children to sleep after a sugar rush so the pastor could preach.

I never knew the cashier's name, but I respected her entrepreneurship to get kids involved in chores as part of money management. Not sure if everyone learned savings is the best path to wealth. We don't need to work forever or reveal our body parts to make over $30 million in a year. Some people need to be needed and mastermind complaints.

Being average is a superpower everybody does not have.

If you have not figured it out by now, God has been after me for a very long time. I realize I am aging with a heap of knowledge gained through decisions that are not all self-made. Lord knows I am doing my best to forge a path and stay afloat. None of us desires to return to God without our purposes fulfilled.

I am patriotic. I am progovernment. I confess it bothers me that America is not utilizing all its talents to generate money. To say I am humbly sitting at Jesus's feet is an understatement. I am alive by the grace of God, and whatever clarity I can provide to any lightworker in training, God, please don't let me fail.

This book is going to weave to and fro through the vernacular and was a heck of a project to explain without a straitjacket. Not everybody is going to understand it because, truthfully, it was not written for everybody. You may retain 3 percent of what you read, but feel free to highlight anything that resonates and buy the book for a friend.

Now, dry your eyes and hold your head up. We are assigned to Earth and have important work to do.

CHAPTER 3

o say, can you sea

Three times a week, before work, Citta would stop at any Catholic church and pray: "God, please give me the strength to get through the day. Help me not to curse. Don't let me die early. I know You protect fools. Thank You for my family. Show me my enemies. Give the dead peace. Amen."

And then, temptation would set in. Truth is, Citta is not afraid of death. One day it will happen. It happens to everybody born of a woman or as it is written. We have to live enjoying the moment with some applied logic toward longevity and happiness. Eat right. Drink filtered water, not necessarily bottled. Maintain a range of motion. Confess our sins as needed. If a glass of red wine helps, cheers!

True, if you don't launch your mind, you remain still. Effortlessly advance your spirit before your feet, and daily think outside the box. Between that and this, we all have these moments of dreaming our worth to be beyond Fabergé eggs, only to wake up feeling limited. Eyes closed, we extend our arms and fly. Eyes open, we are grounded by gravity, saving cash to buy a ticket to venture in flight.

I suppose, depending on what we envision, we manifest winners and losers, educating ourselves through chosen or assigned faith. Eliminating distractions with discipline should be the norm, but at times, it seems school, music, and the Bible are a common denominator of drumbeats.

These tools (as named above) easily become a series of survival skills, depending on our interpretations. We memorize the emotion to relive the feeling. If we jumped intellectual hurdles, we'd be entrepreneurs with no loans and fees to pay off for being smart first. Then accrued income post overhead could be a nest egg for decades. Instead, we spend time seeing the glass ceiling and competitively complain about a lack of excellence.

God has been watching you since you were a child. Certainly, He has bigger plans for you than where you are right now. Let me teach you how I know.

I've never seen Satan in the pews of a Catholic church. You know, where open eyes black over. That level of truth is as rare as the light(s) of visitation. Not sure which dimensions intermingle because observation is not the same and as well studied. I confess it is getting harder for even me to separate the Indigo from the Crystal and the Starseed from the Rainbow. Perhaps we select our parents based on heaven's spectrum and then arrive to reign. We, being magnetic life-puzzle shapes, can either draw our "peace" near or push our "peace" far to occupy space toward a greater future.

The floating light or specks, not to be confused with floaters from a sugary diet, are only embraced by the strong or select few. You, like Citta, are gifted, not crazy. On pause, not eliminated. You are not going to arrive at the hotel to find a Prince or Princess Charming, but you will be set aside and matured to become a pot of gold.

It is my opinion that you are an ongoing growing vine. Never quite finished but able to explain your past better than your future.

Every December we present gifts to celebrate life openly and collectively. As a season of lights, one religion and custom to another, we are accurate and necessary but underdeveloped due to time management.

Not all things in life are taught in classrooms. I just found out the back of the toaster has removeable trays for crumbs.

My point: if you only view people at face value, you will easily miss their processes, strengths, and wisdom. Not everyone knows the options for their futures. They apply for the opportunities to live them but truly fear the goodness they can spread. You are the gift and what you give during the holiday for some is just what they wanted, but what do you want? Why do you ask for something and then shy away from what you asked for as if you don't deserve it?

We move in a world where children are born with their spirit eyes open. Pyramids are still in the same pattern as the stars in the sky, while we who walk the earth remain baffled. This of course is right up there with no dinosaurs in the Bible, but we are surrounded by the bones in the dirt. Something is going on, and then there is something bigger than that.

Whatever you hear calling you in your spiritual slumber state is probably a dispatched angel from God testing your intention. Hearing is different from listening and listening requires discernment. Because no one knows what you are thinking until you open your mouth, apparently testing your hearing and sight in the school curriculum elevates you toward a greater purpose.

As your friend, let me try to explain slower; because once you understand, you can't be robbed.

We label children as prodigy, ADD, ADHD, OCD, Aspie, Indigo, Crystal, Star, or Rainbow or diagnose Down syndrome, dyslexia, and Tourette's. We set them apart for special training and decrease their comprehension to what can be controlled because if they exceed our familiar understanding, we cannot teach or challenge them.

Unnecessary cough medicine might make children sleepy, but as direct, unfabricated, bored messengers (who we prayed for), they (our beautiful and handsome children) are not going to waste time in an attempt to fall short generating truth, defending cause, distributing charity, or earning income. As souls to erase corruption, we blame our faith in children on man-made immunization, overlooking our participation in their nutrition, dietary consumption, processed foods, and/or recipes.

We do not call children millionaires because our format of income is loyal to time. We are educated to be career employees, doctors, nurses, or police, but our children via concentration exceed our expectations.

Based on their expertise and technology, the variety of rivers they can draw wealth from appears endless.

The sharpest tool in the shed is still untouched because we know iron sharpens iron. But yeah, OK, we take an iron pill because we don't want to be skilled nutritionists or farmers. We don't want to learn language to increase distribution of products. We just want to glide through time on stealth.

CHAPTER 4

heir to here

Nothing in existence was created or matures without faith. If the church is a hospital, both church and hospital are closing because the evidence of God is in generations of people not going to church. They don't want to learn scripture because the Word is being manipulated, if not abused, for guilty responses or personal financial gain. The text is memorized but not taught. This is separate from the concordance guide.

Tithe covers bills. If you want or plan to come back to church next week, pay the tithe. If you don't buy a patch of land, build a solar-powered tiny-home village, and tap into a free-flowing water source, unfortunate people will never be independent from social services. There are plenty of people desiring citizenship who can learn to earn while rebuilding land affected by natural disasters.

Second chances and reform should be an option for everybody incarcerated, certainly everybody who is a veteran. If the states became individual territories, the borders and boundaries would deplete, and our enemies could easily conquer resources and landmarks. Drilling America into an unpayable debt in or out of internationally owned or former American land taxes or tolls should not be an option because very few states are not borrowing from tourist cities to make ends meet.

If you get bamboozled out of the right to vote, what other freedoms go with it?

The math of Noah's ark for the sizes of the animals; the magi venturing to see Jesus as a toddler, not an infant; Sarah's age at pregnancy on the original calendar, even if you use the metric system; and Jesus born of a manless seed do not add up. No disrespect, but make it make sense! We have transparent evidence of God and Jesus because we cannot breathe on our own. So are we talking spirits in flesh bodies? Have we made religion mystical, imagining God, the Lord, and Jesus as Savior in human form because we are humans? Are we safeguarding potential because with awareness comes accountability? Is church a nonprofit business only, or are we empowering the congregation to manifest God as unlimited power?

The same people have always been there in church. They don't graduate and rarely demonstrate Jesus without in-house competitive funding. We perish without vision and dream with lazy hands. We don't intermingle worship. We study Jesus because man cannot control the rising of the sun or the setting of the same, and then we start over without advancing, or getting out of the seat, as a generational ownership or curse. Being unhealed on purpose is almost as bad as cutting off the ends of the ham in the large pot. The spiritual people are outside the building, suffering from church hurt or wounds, and the people inside the church are religious.

Allow me to be transparent and speak to you the way I write. "Whatever you don't use, you lose" is a phrase assigned to things, not people. Church is losing the soul battle based on the theory "Study as I did to think behind my progress, not advance before me, because I came first." Who in their right mind wants to follow a leader on a loop path when Jesus is waiting for a bride?

Technology never falls asleep, and everything connected to it is launching into the future, except the church. Large cities are positioning themselves to re-evaluate the distribution of monetary overflow. Inflation is at the front of everybody's finances. So if God sent a new gene toward genius, He'd have every right to change His mind about us. If you want to move the body, you talk to the head, and it seems a lot of clergy have private planes when people can't afford to eat or pay rent.

From 2020 to 2022, the world changed with you on it. Today, post COVID-19 (a.k.a. the business-as-usual apocalypse), God included you in His plan. It is His goal for you to survive. He must need you to make it to the next level in life but not with the same pattern from yesterday. It is time for you to restart, to improve yourself, what you use, and how you use it.

Open your eyes.

Drugs in the street temporarily eliminate pain. You are unquestionably a fascinating human being, sheltered from your own power by the division of what you imagine. (It is easier to excuse yourself from the table with an empty dinner plate when you really do not want to participate in the table conversation.) The illusion in your unchallenged mind would have you believe people with fast sneakers can outrun the law and the shoebox money is still on the untarred roof. That is as true as rabbits laying jelly beans.

We dress it up, and we make it happen based on business, not truth.

I encourage you to live. The awakening of you is a forever lesson. It will not happen in one day. You will have days of revelation that sometimes happen as déjà vu. When you look back (because in your quiet time, you'll probably have no choice), you will find all the puzzle pieces fit. Meanwhile, pray "return to sender" for everything *bad* anybody wants to give you for free. When the dark-gray shadows come and the bright shadows reach out, stay sane! Pray God protects you from danger seen and unseen. Ask Jesus to bless your family, those who like you and those who don't, your assigned poisonous, backstabbing Judases included. Whether you did evil in your life or not, ask for for-giveness and allow yourself to heal.

That forgiveness part is very important. Church hurt should not be normalized.

CHAPTER 5

believe in life

Citta…

That man, every Saturday, would run. Not like a cadence, not like the others. Citta would see him. Dream of him. But the chaos to "keep your mind right" is a trip. You cannot be who anyone wants or who everybody needs. The purpose of prayer for some is never to attract a beggar spirit. He is God; He created everything in seven days, and we still have not found it all.

Meanwhile, strive to be a better you.

At an age of minty paste in a red jar (you're not supposed to eat), Citta would draw a large circle on paper and colorful dots in the circle. Large circle. Dots. Didn't matter the size of the paper. Mini circles in the large circle. Finally in view of the obsession, Citta's mom asked, "What are you drawing?"

"It's you, Mommie" was probably not a normal response. 'Twas the truth, though.

Her momma, between making Sunday sauce from scratch, scheduled the appointment with the one-stop, cure-all physician. The doctor said, "Citta was born with her eyes open. This is what she remembers seeing from the inside."

Oh great! Young, gifted, and bored with no teacher to navigate the "unexplainable this." What has changed?

People *never* tell you about the part where the family baton falls in your lap, your bones ache, you gain weight being still. Sweat comes because you are thinking about a cup of sugar and look ageless! You fall asleep with your clothes on and forget to take your meds on time.

Every so often, you've gotta take everything off. Lies and the wait of the world included. Look at the scars that make you kings and queens, peculiar and strong.

Your grandparents know your life before you do. They know about the fish and lost-tooth dream(s). They know why the bird comes to or in the house window. If you've ever found favor with your grandparent(s), appreciate what you accomplished. You've done a lot alone under their watchful guardianship without notepad or internet.

What you learn from them is your inheritance. For this alone, be grateful and proud.

CHAPTER 6

reignbeau

"So, how does this work?"

"Ha, you mean my life? Don't you know I am the chameleon?" Citta said. She felt like she was talking to a pillar of truth, but you've gotta be careful of the pedestals you put people on. Words are building blocks. Those who own your mind through words can surely whisper in the rent-free brain space and tear everything in you all the way down.

He replied, "You will never be happy with just one person." And Citta wondered if it were true. If that seed, just planted, would grow from the ear gate toward an unplanned thought.

Is this why they say you should seek God for yourself?

Truth be told, you either merge your lane to survive, or you don't. Natural disaster, community unity, or not. These dreams we dream, two point five kids at age twenty-five with a spouse who is not sitting up under you, needy all the time. Good hair and pretty hands, calloused by effort. I don't know any partner who purposely wants to be saddened by a relationship. You hope the person who gives out club flyers is not 100 percent gay and you have a chance at a shot without being offensive or rude. Never happens, but still, the vision of love sends people into work whistling like you and your perfect mate discovered why the garage is not attached to the house.

"No, sir," Citta said. "I am well aware I am going to be single most of my life." It was as if you could hear the music and cheers from a latex ballroom in the background. Value as a woman is complicated because one foot is on Earth and the other a fantasy taboo of everything else. We don't have names. We don't have rights. We are just endlessly servicing pleasure or responsibility until empty, making money along the way so as not to live check to check. We are starting to look like rubber-stamp Stepford wives. Smart but not unique. We give advice between the questionably unanointed, daily passing God in the street. You watch TV for the programs; others watch for messages as if the busyness of life purposely makes one unfocused.

Together the world goes around. But how do you follow up with angels unaware day after day? Find a quiet place? Pray? Be nice to everybody you know?

Where you volunteer to lay your life down, be it in the trusting place of associates who use you as an alibi or not, don't mistake the people around you as friends. Consequences from words are not the same as actions from invisible pressure. Proving innocence is hard. Not all mistakes can be fixed.

If you believe it is better to be by yourself to grow your mind and set your goals, you are probably right. That is good for you.

We are not all born to be married, and Citta missed having friends, sometimes. The suicidal semicolons who were forced to hide under their beds in shame and the life-ending periods who just wanted their pain to end. Failing suicide has lifelong effects. Your mind has to remain determined to win life. We are not all dealt a perfect, two-parent-home starting line. Wealth distributed to someone who cannot manage money is the fastest way to blow cash. It happens. Yes, it is bad to owe money, but how else can you build credit, knowing the interest on a payday loan can leave you homeless?

We (you, me, all of us) have been a thousand people in a thousand lifetimes. All zodiac signs, various ages. Those who walk on water always know they are stepping in an unfamiliar place on purpose. We listen to intuition and believe everything bad in life eventually turns around for good.

You don't need to live in California, Georgia, New York, or Texas to find fame and fortune. Whatever effort you apply, wherever you live, apply yourself as the foundation of your future.

The entourage, VIPs, and the grand illusionist may show up for your big event. Yes, expect a day when God pulls back the world curtain to say, "Look at my child," that whatever in your life you have not addressed will be right beside you. I kid you not; the darkness and all its nasty secrets do come to light.

Whatever demon you've gotta fight on a daily basis will either roll to the next available soul, remain unaddressed but not necessarily silent, or step out onstage when you step out. The voice or temptation comes to everybody, and it is easy to lose hope if no one described to you *who God could be.* No one sat you down and explained, "Whatever you do, do well; *God needs you to dream BIGGER.*" He has the power to magnify your lifestyle simply by giving you a present moment.

I don't know how life unfolds for Muslims who follow the Moon or Jews who follow the Star, but Christians, pure in heart, following the Son, are on every winning award show, thanking God if they cannot say Jesus on TV. Acceptance speeches are written the day people decide their purposes, not the day they are nominated.

Allow yourself to become more than what you are now. If Jesus breathed into man to start life, then it would make sense that you are a fraction of the whole. I mean, learn CPR to save your family with your own breath.

CHAPTER 7

unscathed

There are three things I need to tell you:

1. If somebody tells you they don't know how to cook, it does not mean they do not know how to fish.

2. Don't hear what you want to hear when people talk to you. Not everybody is going to fit in the dotted lines of the coloring book. Stay away from real, live people who cast no image in mirrors. If you know your potential *and* your power, call out evil before it lands.

3. God will not allow you to be abused, and it never goes unaddressed. He has no problem cutting holes in pockets.

GOD SAW YOU WHEN you had to make the decision of surgery. God can count all your stitches. God saw your tissue expanders, implants, and drains. God saw you take the pills the day you tried to die. God saw you the day the repairman made a professional error. God saw you the day you had the mayo-only sandwich. God can wipe your bullied tears. God can erase fears and deliver you from evil. God can make you temporarily rich or hungry to bless people. God can make you temporarily poor so you understand the strength you were born with. God is not practicing being God. God has no days off.

As well as God knows you, you should return the favor and learn Him.

People of every faith pray for a safe return before they leave the house. If you live alone and your mind is paranormally strong enough to bend spoons, do that. But pray once a day or week to cover you to or until the next period of time. There is really no way for God to learn your heart if your mouth is shut.

Also…

When you ask God, Allah, Jesus, Buddha, or the rabbi to reveal things, you need to be anchored with more than an altar call and face-down repentance for what is around you that you can't physically see as you become spiritually aware.

This includes fangs, shadows, superstitions, spilled water, table salt, Saint Anthony for things lost, human people who growl, crazy people who are sane, sane people who scream, hands that smell like sanitizer, alcoholics filled with wisdom, folks with degrees who ain't street smart, kids who speak the future through authority, undefined logic, the begging angel who comes on payday, guilt at tax time, man-made fear, traditional ignorance, lucky numbers that highlight and float, all the dimensions, strings of life, red-cloth protection, the bling that blinds bad spirits, gargoyles on buildings, black salt, names or pictures in freezers, and yes, chicken lips.

All of it, every last bit, is energy capable of being loyal. The dirt you find yourself in and *the seed that is in you* really can defeat all evil. Just keep on living, seeking who God is in your time of trouble. God wants you happy.

Can you pray into goodness? Absolutely *yes*!

CHAPTER 8

this is the that

Adam was an atom, and Eve was the beginning, but the snake stayed and was not cast away from the Tree of Knowledge. At some point what we say can't all be Satan *and* struggle.

Speak to God about what bothers you. If He doesn't move it, if you can't hear Him, then you have the ability to change your circumstance but probably can't see it. Move in the direction where the result glorifies and advances the Kingdom so the angels know where to go. Now is not the time to fill your mind with negativity. In fact, no day ever is.

You want a job? Speak the application. Practice for your interview. Get your clothes ready.

Clean shirt, dark pants, skirt or slacks. Shoes shined, if possible. Appropriate hosiery. One pair of earrings, nothing shiny (studs preferred, not hoops). Wedding band if married but not an engagement ring. Wake up for the job; look for the opportunity.

Stand for the phone interview. Don't sit in a face-to-face interview before the interviewer. Keep panel interviews stress-free.

Know the company, competitor, and industry.

No hmms. No ers. Have your adjectives to describe you ready! Practice being you, but don't sound rehearsed. No bubble gum! No overwhelming perfume. Do not reveal your five-year plan. Use the appropriate résumé to highlight your skills. Know your past tense from present. Answer all questions truthfully. Ask for more responsibility, not necessarily a position in management. Most of all, don't be late or quit.

Always move ambition laterally. It is better to have a job and get a new job than to appear lazy when not fresh out of school. If you *ever* have an uncomfortable issue at work, document everything in writing.

The opportunities in life that are for you should not pass you by.

CHAPTER 9

it will dew

I t is hard to see people and not tell them what you see. You are going to be famous; you will have awards; you should finish school and not use a horoscope or an astrology chart as an entertainment option.

Citta met men who were not kind. One after the other. God being a jealous God watched her loyalty, her endurance in spite of the disrespect. When people think your father is deceased, the roar in their jungle should not define you. For this reason alone, *you matter to God*!

Never believe an eagle can teach a lion to fly. The lion cub that never hears a roar will lie dormant, believing it is simply wingless and unclaimed, until it stubs its toe by accident.

A woman might birth nations, but the man's body makes the Y chromosome. The abnormal use of the procreation process increases the probability of the X chromosome or removal of the Y, which is why men of various ethnicities and ages are in jail. It is not population control. People are incarcerated for being smart. Don't believe me? Weed is a stock filling the financial gap like a farm. It should no longer be considered a crime.

It is no secret men empower communities. Men earn the big piece of chicken, and if Father is absent, give it to Mother. If Mother and Father have gone on to glory, then divide your money like a dinner plate. Half to savings, a quarter to spend, and a quarter for emergencies. *Never give away what you are supposed to have.*

You earn respect and trust. You never let anyone steal your dignity. No human can fill the void in another human. That only leads to dependency.

Liquid, powder, liquor, pill, or strange smoke—direct or by supplier—is not a gym you want to take your mind to. The genius of a man or woman alters out of boredom. We use lovers as slot holders. But no lover can protect you from yourself. No church can answer all questions. No hospital can cure death.

We are locked in time. You can mark it; extend it in different forms, such as history or legacy, to remain in it; and create timeless masterpieces of art, music, or dance to never leave it. Physically, we come and go, recycling energy, elevating in frequency, delayed but ever learning.

You have to be open to the life you want. Without time, we are current, nothing and everything. You will be who you think you are.

CHAPTER 10

oil and hinges

Citta invested time trying to turn frogs into her prince.

She fell asleep, waking to a TV preacher hollering, "If you can hear my voice, come out of the closet and get yourself to church." She had to go to this church. It was a goal to walk to the building on foot as if she were Jewish en route to the Temple. She, like most, wanted to be loyal and radical, but her heart was empty. She moved out from Mother's house, defended her country in war, met a man, pushed out a baby, and moved back to Mother's house.

For her, there seemed to be no mate. No one she could play out as a "slow-motion lover" in her mind. She desired the right man, eventually three men individually, but they played the same game, that of a player. So there was no adult embrace at the end of the day.

Because we are taught to never outthink the system, we just kind of roll with it. You observe and do as you are told unless you are the boss and your name is on the door. You're not supposed to date your coworker, but you do. Not supposed to sleep with the owner, but you have. And you got fired for either standing up, lying down, or being who you are without apology. Yeah, bizarre things happen, and you want to be protected from shenanigans but not at the cost of being vulnerable or stupid, believing you are immortal.

Karma is karma. Unloved is not the same as "loved but not in a relationship." No matter where you are in life, you are loved. Cancer patients are loved. HIV patients are loved. For some, love is the hardest thing to admit, but *please don't ever end your life based on how someone treats or treated you*. You cannot give love if you do not have it for yourself.

I noticed that when you tell people your sexual preference, people get mad when you never invite them to your lesbian, bisexual, transgender, gay, or even straight bedroom. Citta longed to be on the good side of an attractive commitment. Frankly, if you're going to "get your feet done" and nobody ever intimately licks them by meaningful accident, somebody ain't living up to their potential. Honey, lemme tell you: God sees everything. What you like, don't like, did *and* didn't do.

We're humans, and *how we are touched is life.* The people who speak life make us better people. Keep them!

Citta, with all her heart, got on the plane, landed, and had her stuff held at ransom by land movers for an extra $3,000 in twenty-four hours, which resulted in a Better Business Bureau complaint. She moved in, groceries were put in the fridge, storm lights came, and plan A spun into plan C quickly.

She sat at a man's feet with questions, but as a single parent, you can't ask a man of the cloth questions. Simply put, you have too much unseen oil from Aaron's beard on you to do that.

You request an elder, who never comes. And you want to grow in God because you're eager to be obedient. And you're supposed to give flowers to people while they are living. All this would be very simple if the man of the church house could just answer questions.

Citta, not knowing the protocol to get holy water from the spout during Catholic service, was now in a position where she could hear God. She could see the

Spirit; she could not see man. She was not blind. Angels were at the ready, but something unusual happened.

The genres paid to disrespect women do not increase population. Each global tour becomes conversational but not maximally profitable. If we lose the freedom of the internet with or without a blackout, we lose everything America has to offer, becoming submissive to competitors who may be more foe than friend.

It is not just bizarre for America to lose our number one slot. It is out of order!

Once you manifest as *chosen*, it changes your whole life. It is only then that you should expect jealousy to grow you because the experience will not fail. Let nothing deplete the power of your union.

Citta thought gifted folk looked out for each other and the church did not eat their young. She thought the Bible, as in bi/able of a spiritual and physical aspect of power, was not taught as such. So collectively, now we all have questions about the accuracy of elevation. Who promotes whom, how "the unexplainable accurate," which we often identify as prophetic, is considered magic, witchcraft, or sorcery by Christians because Christians promote the "get behind me" logic for everything outside church. Technically, accuracy from both is the same thing. I am not promoting black magic or voodoo or leaving food out for the absent. I will say, I have friends who are experts in what they believe and have warned me of unkindness in advance for *free*. They did not have to do it, but I am grateful they did.

Church hurt was a scar, the size of a two-year red-hue letter. And Citta could no longer be ministered in the church building, through music, or walk through town with head held high. She curled in the fetal position with no more tears to shed. Police knocked for wellness checks. Did she own weapons? Would she harm herself or worse? Seems that because she could not pick the right man or find a teacher without appearing crazy, God heard her and *showed up*.

"God, I thought I was doing right…growing right. I divorced my parents' protection and everything familiar to follow You so my family could mature without hate. If you can hear me, send me the Teacher of my pastor."

Hell landed on her, with her kid in the house. Hell landed on her in church hurt. Landed as chaos in which neighbors to trust. Landed while borrowing money, living in a car, using a local superstore's bathroom in the midnight hour. Landed while she bathed her child in the twenty-four-hour Laundromat so he would never miss school, sleeping on layers of blankets in the back seat, always having clean clothes.

Citta repented for much, but she was never angry at God. She was prophetic perhaps but often spoke prematurely. It was scary for some, so she became wiser but talked less. Favor will terminate you from a job and ban you from the church premises, but it never appears as an uplifting promotion or protection when it happens. It is all a process.

Her child's education altered to another path. As intellectual wonders, children get bullied in school. Without a sheet of paper that states "completion," any cub's roar will project as underdeveloped. We loop children back into classrooms as if they are not currently suffering from PTSD, but we don't quit work to keep them safe. If the real lions of the world ever stop breathing, what cub can survive on its own?

CHAPTER 11

you so fly

Today is a blessing designed just for you.

Learn to think differently. Guard your ear gate. Don't speak out of turn unless you can't hold it. Never let someone tell you something is foolproof. Even in an emergency, when you ask for help, help may not come in time. When you think wrong, you can trip, break a leg, or twist an ankle but keep on living.

The success of you is major because it is never finished. If you have a spot on your lung, it could very well be a fluke, and you will worry and cry and cry and worry, missing the best days of your life.

Time has come twice for Citta to go home. Rent a truck, humble head, and return to parents with failed plans to be independent chasing Jesus. She rebuilt her life up from hard times, with no husband, no boy-friend.

It is hard to love the man who won't let you forget your past. It is hard to love the man who does not believe he can have a future with you. It is hard to embrace everybody who wants you to have the right man, and only God shows up.

Love is not money. Love is not fame. If God is the only man sitting right beside you, let Him sit.

Give Him what He wants!

Citta loved that He loved the intimacy of prayer, and Citta loved that she had access to Him but hated that He decided not to visit her every day or more than once a day, including overnight. Knowing Citta would never be at the top of her game with Him (by His choice, of course), something or someone had Him locked into routine. It was obviously more important for Him to be absent to her, but respectfully.

If He with a camera on His house and those loyal by oath feared for His life, *and* He failed to come home…

If He were in the care of a young person, who had to see Him every night to understand His Word, how His commitment is His bond, or how real love never fades…

Even if He had a woman at home as the meal and women on the side as snacks and He needed to be available to all because He stays hungry for hot toothpick samples to protect the family…

Citta understood.

He keeps His mouth shut and plays His cards close to his chest with a front-row seat to many in the struggle.

If you woke up every morning thinking about a good person who believes you are the most deserving partner playing your heart cheap to the highest bidder, you would want someone to step in. Walk you through the experience of better.

My question to the church is simple. If Jesus wore a ring on the fifth finger, would we love, respect, and honor Him more? Would we stand united, defend the oath and vow, or close doors preventing all people who don't look or act like us to know or invest in Him?

They say they don't make women like Citta anymore. Maybe they do; maybe they don't. Those of us outside the four walls, we were raised believing the greatest power on Earth is the God Father and the greatest wisdom falls from the lips of grandmothers who cook in the kitchen. Should both images go home to glory and we all remain silent, the belief of Jesus will die because we were not man or woman enough to protect Him.

Maybe we are not scared enough to believe we can wake up and lose the freedom to worship at a church, mosque, or temple. Once you're in Jesus's family, man can't undo your faith, so the power of Him should remain ongoing. We dream to be winners in all things, the shero/hero in all movies, projecting truth with the best luxuries of life. It is our nature to speak power as protection. Perhaps God watches over all of us, waiting for us to whisper like morning crows, looking up for facial recognition, and from that level of loyalty comes extended life.

We are late returning to church in deed, in person, in talent, and online. Generations of dreams are being funeralized by the internet, and people are turning their hearts away from God. They are angry about change that is not familiar.

You, who seek Christ, I believe you will be all right. I encourage you to pursue Jesus so you survive dark days and shine in experience and evidence that He exists. I sincerely pray that your hands not be idle and restoration (in this lifetime) not escape you.

If it sounds like I am asking everybody on Earth to collectively step up for Jesus like He is a boss, *I am*.

God's name is on American money, and daily I hope we don't fail Him. This book is eighteen years of a very long labyrinth, proof and evidence you will score big in life no matter what your name is.

It is easy to fall into foolish traps that play the ends against the middle. When people appear to dislike you, it is because your intelligence, wealth, endurance, and health unfold an ability to manifest Jesus in public. Your power is not your skin tone. *Your power is your focus.* Religion is predictable. Your spirit is not. Don't be silent when He calls you on purpose.

Keep Growing
Keep Living
Keep Talking
Move Your Bones
Drink Water
Dream *Big*
Forgive; Don't Forget
Practice Your Best You
Become the Leader You Need
Love Those Who Love You, But Love You First
Prevent Generational Mistakes
Accept All Lessons
Honor Your Soul-Mind Unconditionally
Wherever You Are, Be Who God Made

"And I saw the holy city, new Jerusalem, coming down out of heaven from God, prepared as a bride adorned for her husband." (Revelation 21:2, RSV). Amen.

CPSIA information can be obtained
at www.ICGtesting.com
Printed in the USA
LVHW011050170523
747209LV00007B/580